BEING BAD
FOR THE
BABY-SITTER

Other Little Apple Paperbacks
you will enjoy:

Good Grief . . . Third Grade
Colleen O'Shaughnessy McKenna

Striped Ice Cream
Joan M. Lexau

Class Clown
Johanna Hurwitz

Werewolves Don't Go to Summer Camp
Debra Dadey and Marcia Jones

BEING BAD
FOR THE
BABY-SITTER

Richard Tulloch

Interior illustrations by Coral Tulloch

A
LITTLE APPLE
PAPERBACK

SCHOLASTIC INC.
New York Toronto London Auckland Sydney

ISBN 0-590-46061-7

12 11 10 9 8 7 6 5 4 3 2 1   4 5 6 7 8 9/9

Printed in the U.S.A.   40

First Scholastic printing, July 1994

Author's dedication
For Sarah

Illustrator's dedication
To Geoff De Groen

BEING BAD
FOR THE
BABY-SITTER

One night Jane's mother was going out to
see a movie. Jane wanted to see the movie
too, but Jane's mother said no, the movie
wasn't suitable for Jane at all because it
was one of those movies for grown-ups
which Jane would find quite boring. Be-
sides which, it might have blood and scary
stuff that would give Jane nightmares.

Jane started to say that she liked movies with blood and scary stuff, but Jane's mother said Jane had the school swimming carnival tomorrow and needed a good night's sleep. So she had to stay home. With a baby-sitter.

Jane hated baby-sitters.

Before the baby-sitter arrived, Jane had to have an early dinner and an extra long bath and brush her teeth and put on her pajamas and get tucked into bed after only a short story while it wasn't even dark outside. Just so the baby-sitter wouldn't have any trouble.

The baby-sitter who came that night to look after Jane was a new one that Jane didn't know. She'd never been to Jane's house before. Her name was Marilyn.

Marilyn wore glasses and a yellow cardigan and carried a thick library book.

"Be good for Marilyn, Jane," said Jane's mother as she went out the door. But Jane just scowled her grumpiest scowl and said nothing.

That was because Jane was making up a plan which went like this:

Tonight I'm going to be really, really bad for Marilyn, because then she'll never want to come back here. And she'll tell all the other baby-sitters how bad I am. So none of the other baby-sitters will want to come here and then I won't have to have a baby-sitter ever again, and instead I'll be able to go and see movies with blood and scary stuff.

And as soon as her mother's car was out
of the driveway and around the corner,
Jane began being really, really bad.

She waited in bed until Marilyn was just sitting down in her chair in the living room to read her thick library book.

"Marilyn!" called Jane.

"What is it?" asked Marilyn.

"I'm thirsty," said Jane.

"Oh," said Marilyn.

So Marilyn went to the kitchen and half a minute later she brought Jane a drink of water. The water looked good, and Marilyn had poured it into a real grown-up's glass with an ice cube clinking in it. But Jane's plan was to be bad.

"Water!" said Jane. "Yuck!" And she spilled the water on the floor and pretended it was an accident.

"Oh, that was bad luck," said Marilyn.

She cleaned up the water with a towel
and brought Jane a glass of orange juice
which Jane drank without even saying
thank you.

Then she waited in bed until Marilyn sat down in her chair in the living room and went back to reading her thick library book.

"Marilyn!" called Jane.

"What is it?" asked Marilyn.

"I'm hungry," said Jane.

"Oh," said Marilyn.

So Marilyn went to the kitchen and made Jane a cheese and lettuce sandwich, decorated with a sprig of parsley. The sandwich looked very good. But Jane's plan was to be bad.

"Cheese and lettuce!" said Jane. "Yuck!"
And she knocked the sandwich off its
plate and pretended it was an accident.

"Oh, that was bad luck," said Marilyn.

Marilyn cleaned up the mess and brought Jane a new sandwich made with raspberry jam which Jane ate without even saying thank you.

Then she waited until Marilyn sat down in her chair in the living room and went back to reading her thick library book.

"Marilyn!" called Jane.

"What is it?" asked Marilyn.

"I feel sick," groaned Jane.

"Oh," said Marilyn. "What sort of sick?"

"I think it's gastric," said Jane, clutching her head.

"Isn't gastric something you get in your tummy?" asked Marilyn.

"Oh, it's in my tummy too, of course," said Jane quickly, "but I get this special really bad gastric that goes all the way up to my head. And if I don't get urgent medical attention I'm liable to throw up."

"Oh, really?" said Marilyn.

"All over the carpet," added Jane.

Marilyn brought Jane a wet cloth to hold on her gastric head and a basin to put beside the bed in case she had to throw up. She took Jane's temperature with the thermometer and rested her hand on Jane's forehead.

Her hand felt cool and comfortable, but Jane's plan was to be bad.

"Get your hand off me!" snapped Jane. "Can't you see I'm sick?"

"I'm sorry," said Marilyn, blushing. And she backed awkwardly out of the bedroom with a strange, hurt expression on her face.

Then she sat down in her chair in the living room and went back to reading her thick library book.

Jane tried to think what she could do next to be bad for Marilyn. It took a long time, but at last she thought of a good idea.

"Marilyn!" called Jane.

"What is it?" asked Marilyn.

"There's a bee in my room!" said Jane.

"Oh," said Marilyn.

She rolled up a newspaper and switched on the light in Jane's bedroom.

"Where is the bee?" she asked.

"Behind the wardrobe," said Jane.

Marilyn tried to look behind the wardrobe but it was too dark.

"Did you see it go in there?" asked Marilyn.

"Er, no," said Jane, "but I heard it in there buzzing. And any moment now it could fly out and sting me. You'd better move the wardrobe and swat it."

The wardrobe was heavy. Marilyn couldn't move it until she'd taken all the clothes and drawers out and piled them up in the middle of the room. Jane wouldn't even help, because her plan was to be bad.

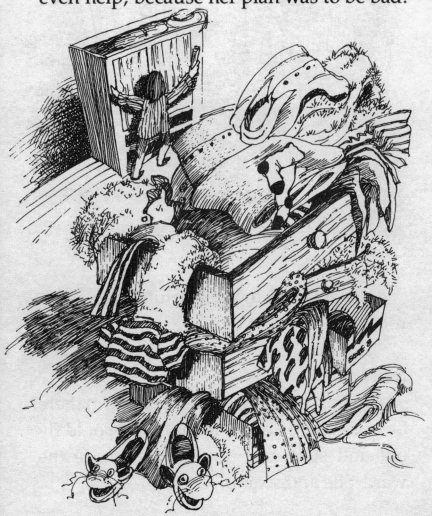

She pretended to be scared of the bee and still sick with her gastric head. She sat up in bed with the sheet pulled up to her chin and watched as Marilyn struggled and strained and finally moved the wardrobe out from the wall.

There was no bee.

"Maybe it just flew out the window," said Jane.

"Let's hope so," said Marilyn, with her teeth pressed tight together.

And after she'd moved the wardrobe back against the wall, she replaced all the drawers and hung up all the clothes again and switched out the light.

Then she sat down in her chair in the living room and went back to reading her thick library book.

It took a very long time for Jane to think up her next bad idea, but when she did, it went like this . . .

"Marilyn!" called Jane, very softly.

"What is it?" asked Marilyn.

"Marilyn!" hissed Jane, in her very loudest whisper, "I just saw a burglar, climbing past my window up onto our roof."

"Oh," said Marilyn. "Are you sure?"

"Of course I'm sure," said Jane. "I saw him. He was all dressed in a black burglar suit and he's planning to come down our chimney and steal all our famous paintings and all Mommy's valuable jewels. So you'd better climb up there and get him down right now!"

Marilyn looked at Jane in a funny way, but she didn't say anything. Then she went outside with a ladder and a flashlight. She climbed up onto the roof and carefully shone the flashlight around the edge.

After a little while she called, "Jane, I can't see any burglar up here."

"I think I just saw him swing on a rope over to our neighbor's house," said Jane. "You'd better come down now and call the police, Marilyn."

And then Jane did a very bad thing.
She took the ladder away. And waited to
see what Marilyn would do.

And waited. And waited.

"What's the matter, Marilyn?" said Jane. "We can't have a baby-sitter stuck up on our roof all night. People will think you're a burglar. Come on down right now!"

But Marilyn didn't come down.

Instead Jane heard a sniffling sound coming from the roof. Then it was quiet again. Then there was a sob.

"Marilyn?" said Jane.

But there was no more sound.

Jane put the ladder back against the side of the house, climbed up, and looked over the edge of the roof. Marilyn was sitting right up on top, holding her head in her hands.

Jane crawled up the side of the roof until she could sit up on top beside her.

"What's the matter, Marilyn?" she asked. "Are you crying?"

Marilyn took off her glasses and wiped her eyes with the corner of her yellow cardigan.

"You know, Jane," she sniffed, "this is the first time I've ever been a baby-sitter. I wanted to be a good one. But now I know I'm really hopeless at it. I'm never going to be a baby-sitter ever again."

"Why not?" asked Jane.

"Because you've been playing tricks on me all night and treating me as if I'm really stupid. I don't know why you hate me so much."

And she burst into a flood of tears.

Jane knew then that her plan had worked and Marilyn would never come back and baby-sit at her house again. But she didn't feel pleased about it at all.

Instead, she felt a lump growing in the back of her throat and her hands were all hot and sticky. She felt bad about the things she'd said and done, and she wanted more than anything to say something that would make Marilyn stop crying. But she didn't know what to say.

"Marilyn?" said Jane.

"What is it?" sniffed Marilyn.

"Can you make hot chocolate?" asked Jane.

"No!" said Marilyn.

"I can," said Jane. "Let's get down and have some."

She climbed down off the roof and then held the ladder steady while Marilyn climbed down after her.

Jane made two cups of hot chocolate and gave one to Marilyn and drank the other one herself.

And they started to talk.

Jane told Marilyn all about her friends
and teachers at school and books she liked
to read and her favorite show on TV and
showed her the scab on her elbow where
she'd scraped it when she fell off her bike
last Tuesday.

Marilyn told Jane about the house where she lived when she was a child and about her dog called Norman and her boyfriend who was away in Indonesia on business until June the sixteenth.

Then Marilyn read Jane a chapter out of her thick library book, which turned out to be not at all boring. It was a grown-up's book which had blood and scary stuff in it.

At last Jane said, "Well, it's been nice meeting you, Marilyn, but I have to go to bed now. I've got the school swimming carnival tomorrow and I need a good night's sleep."

So Marilyn tucked her into bed and switched out the light, and then sat down in the chair in the living room and opened her thick library book again.

"Marilyn," called Jane.

"What is it?" asked Marilyn.

"I think you're a good baby-sitter, Marilyn," said Jane. "Good night."

"Good night, Jane," said Marilyn. "By the way, how's your gastric head?"

And they both laughed.

The next morning, when Jane woke up,
Marilyn was gone.

"Marilyn said you were very good," said Jane's mother, "and she's coming to baby-sit again next Friday. Will that be all right?"

"That will be fine," said Jane. And she meant it, too.